Miranda's Gift

Wayne Simmes

Published by Wayne Simmes, 2024.

While every precaution has been taken in the preparation of this book, the publisher assumes no responsibility for errors or omissions, or for damages resulting from the use of the information contained herein.

MIRANDA'S GIFT

First edition. March 13, 2024.

ISBN: 979-8224437047

Written by Wayne Simmes.

Miranda's Gift

Chapter One – The Discovery

In a quaint town nestled between rolling hills and meandering streams, there lived a curious and imaginative seven-year-old girl named Miranda. With her wide, innocent eyes the color of a cloudless blue sky and a cascade of golden curls that framed her cherubic face, Miranda possessed an allure that endeared her to all in the neighborhood. Little did they know, she harbored a secret that set her apart from the other children.

It all began on a warm summer day when the carnival came to town, painting the streets with vibrant hues and filling the air with the intoxicating scents of spun sugar and buttery popcorn. Miranda, filled with excitement, tugged at her mother's hand, urging her to explore the wonders that awaited them. As they wandered through the lively festivities, Miranda's attention was ensnared by a mysterious man at a makeshift booth performing a mesmerizing shell game.

Miranda keenly observed the man's hands, moving with the swiftness of a striking snake, obscuring the pea from sight. While the crowd stared bewildered, Miranda's imagination took flight, tracking the pea as it danced secretly across the table, vivid as if it glowed. A smile crept across her face as she envisioned the pea, not in the man's grasp, but hiding beneath a shell.

When the eager gambler lifted the shell, Miranda's vision became reality. Gasps rippled through the crowd at the sight of the pea. The operator stared, dumbfounded. Miranda's mother urged her along, but the girl insisted, "The man is cheating, mama!" Her cry resonated, capturing the attention of a nearby officer.

As Miranda and her mother strolled the midway, a booth adorned with colorful balloons seized the girl's interest. Drawn by curiosity, Miranda begged her mother to let her try the game. With rapt focus, Miranda keenly tracked the darts, visualizing their path before they flew. When her turn came, she burst two balloons with ease. But upon inspecting the final dart, she declared it "off balance."

Though the operator insisted otherwise, Miranda's mother encouraged her to proceed. Closing her eyes, the girl envisioned the trajectory of the dart, willing it to hit the mark. When she released it, the balloon burst as if struck by an unseen force. Miranda left triumphant, clutching a prize.

That evening, over dinner, Miranda's father questioned how she conquered such rigged games. Sensing his disbelief, Miranda held her secret close, hoping one day she could reveal her extraordinary gift. For now, the mysteries of her abilities were hers alone to unravel.

Miranda's mother interjected, her voice calm yet defensive. "She won it fair and square, and I only put down three dollars. The man did seem pretty angry, though. And earlier, Miranda caught a man running the shell game cheating. I guess she has very good eyesight."

The explanation hung in the air, but Miranda could sense her father's continued disbelief. Despite knowing the truth – that she possessed the extraordinary ability to move objects with her mind – she wisely chose to keep that astonishing revelation to herself. Maintaining a composed silence, she joined her mother in setting the table, the cheerful clatter of dishes a stark contrast to the unspoken secrets swirling within the room like gathering storm clouds.

Miranda went straight for her room, clutching her prized bear tightly. She placed it on her bed, staring at it thoughtfully. Could it be true? Could she move objects with her mind?

She decided to try. From across the room, she focused on a small toy horse on the shelf. She tried to imagine it moving, envisioning it sliding towards the edge of the shelf.

To her astonishment and delight, it moved.

With a triumphant laugh, Miranda spent the rest of the evening experimenting with objects around her room. It wasn't easy, and it was certainly tiring - but it was real. By bedtime, Miranda knew two things for certain: She had an extraordinary gift and this was only the start of a thrilling adventure."

Chapter Two - Exploration

From that moment forward, Miranda's days became a thrilling exploration of her newfound supernatural abilities. She practiced in secret, moving toys and books with a mere thought, all the while grappling with the extraordinary nature of her mystic powers. The carnival, with its colorful lights and enchanting atmosphere, marked the beginning of a remarkable journey for Miranda, one where the ordinary boundaries of reality blurred into the extraordinary realm of the arcane unknown. Little did she know that her adventures were just beginning, and the world held more mysteries than she could ever imagine.

The message echoed in Miranda's mind as she opened her eyes to the warm morning sun shining through her bedroom window. She sat up in bed, contemplating the cryptic dream and the voice that seemed to know about her abilities.

As much as she wanted to confide in someone – anyone – about her powers, Miranda couldn't shake off the warning from her dream. She knew that if others found out, they would either be afraid of her or try to exploit her powers for their own gain. And neither was a risk she was willing to take.

In the dream, a mysterious figure with iridescent wings emerged from a swirling vortex of colors and spoke to her in a melodic tone that seemed to resonate within her very soul. The voice, like a gentle breeze carrying ancient secrets, cautioned Miranda against sharing the knowledge of her extraordinary abilities.

But as the days passed, Miranda couldn't ignore the growing weight of keeping such a significant secret. Her parents noticed how distant and preoccupied she had become, and they questioned her about it. Miranda was torn between wanting to trust them and fearing their reaction if they found out the truth.

One evening, after dinner, Miranda retreated to her room and closed the door behind her. She sat on the edge of her bed, gazing at a photo of herself with her parents at last year's carnival. A pang of guilt crept into her chest as she thought about how much she was hiding from them.

Suddenly, there was a knock on her door, pulling Miranda out of her thoughts. She quickly wiped away a stray tear before calling out for whoever it was to come in.

It was her mother, and she took a seat next to Miranda on the bed. "Is everything okay, sweetie?" Her mother asked gently.

Miranda hesitated before finally blurting out what had been weighing on her mind for days. "Mom, I have something important to tell you...but I'm scared."

Her mother's expression turned serious as she listened intently. When Miranda finished confessing everything – from discovering her powers at the carnival to using them secretly – there was a long moment of silence between them.

Finally, Miranda's mother spoke softly yet firmly."I won't pretend to understand the full extent of your powers, Miranda. Perhaps it would be best if you did not let anyone else know about this. Miranda told her about the dream and the warning to keep her powers a secret.

One day, as Miranda walked home from school, her attention was drawn to a commotion in the town square. A group of bullies surrounded a timid boy, taunting him and snatching his backpack. The boy's eyes pleaded for help, and Miranda knew she had to act. With a steely determination, she focused her mind on the bullies' backpacks, causing them to mysteriously zip open and spill their contents onto the ground.

Startled by the sudden turn of events, the bullies scrambled to retrieve their belongings, giving the boy a chance to escape. Miranda stood her ground, her eyes flashing with an otherworldly light that sent shivers down the bullies' spines. Without uttering a word, she sent a silent message that resonated with each of them a warning to leave the boy alone.

As the bullies dispersed, Miranda approached the trembling boy and offered him a reassuring smile. She extended a hand to help him gather his scattered belongings.

Chapter Three Unseen Consequences

The next morning, as Miranda glided down the hallway towards her homeroom, she couldn't help but notice a large group of students gathered around the bullies from the previous night. Their voices were raised in excitement and accusation, drawing attention from every corner of the school. "She's a witch, I tell you," one of the bullies exclaimed, his voice dripping with disdain.

Miranda tried to ignore them, but as she passed by, the chant of "witch, witch, witch" followed her like an unwelcome shadow. The crowd seemed to grow larger with each step she took, their stares burning holes into her back. Finally reaching her homeroom, Miranda let out a sigh of relief, only to be followed by a few members of the crowd who lingered outside. Her teacher, Miss Stevens, looked up at the commotion and furrowed her brow in confusion. "What's going on here?" she asked sternly.

"She's a witch," one boy declared boldly.

Miss Stevens raised an eyebrow skeptically. "And who might that be?"

"Miranda," another student piped up. "We saw her moving things with her mind last night. She's got powers."

The room erupted in whispers and hushed conversations. Miss Stevens shook her head disapprovingly before speaking again. "There's no such thing as witches, children. But if there were, I wouldn't want to make one angry with me." She gave a pointed look to the boy who had accused Miranda before adding with a smirk, "They might just turn you into a toad."

After the crowd had dispersed, Miss Stevens leaned in towards Miranda, her brow furrowed with concern. "Can you shed some light on what they are accusing you of?" she asked gently.

Miranda's cheeks flushed with shame as she struggled to come up with a believable answer. "I really don't know," she said softly, trying to hide the quiver in her voice. "I saw some boys bullying Timothy last night. I wanted to help him but I was so little and there were a lot of big boys." She paused, afraid to continue with her lie but knowing it was necessary. "And then for some reason, their backpacks opened spilling the contents on the ground and while they were busy collecting their things, Timothy had a chance to get away from them. I don't know why it happened, perhaps a gust of wind caught them just right. But when they saw me standing there watching them, they must have thought that I had something to do with interrupting their bullying." Miranda's heart raced as she spoke, hoping her story sounded plausible enough to convince her teacher.

"I'll do my best to be your undercover guardian angel at school, but honestly, it might be safer for you to take the scenic route and avoid those trouble-making boys. Unless, of course, you've been secretly brewing potions in your locker," she quipped with a chuckle.

Miranda couldn't help but smile at Miss Stevens' attempt to lighten the situation. She appreciated the teacher's support and understanding, even though the truth remained hidden beneath layers of secrecy. As she settled into her seat, Miranda's mind churned with thoughts of the mysterious warning from her dream and the escalating rumors surrounding her telekinetic abilities.

Throughout the day, whispers followed her in the halls, and curious glances lingered longer than usual. Miranda could sense the shifting currents of suspicion and awe swirling around her, creating an invisible barrier between herself and her classmates. Despite her efforts to blend in and avoid drawing attention, the spotlight of scrutiny seemed determined to cast its unforgiving glare upon her.

As the final bell rang, signaling the end of the school day, Miranda gathered her books and prepared to slip away unnoticed. However, a firm hand on her shoulder halted her escape. Turning around, she found herself face to face with Timothy, the boy she had helped the night before.

The boy shifted his weight nervously, his words tumbling out in a rush. "I didn't get a chance to properly thank you last night," he began.

Miranda smiled kindly but waved away his gratitude. "You have nothing to thank me for. I simply hope those boys will leave you alone now."

The boy's eyes widened in surprise. "But I heard your voice inside my head, warning them to stay away from me. I don't know how you did it, but I'm grateful you did. Roger and Clyde have been making my life a living hell lately. Stealing my lunch money, tearing up my assignments, even getting me in trouble with my teachers."

Miranda's expression turned serious as she offered a solution. "You should report them to the Principal."

The boy shook his head vehemently. "That would only make things worse. But thank you again, for everything." His words were filled with genuine appreciation and Miranda knew she had made a difference in this young boy's life.

As Miranda made her way home, she couldn't shake the feeling of being watched. Glancing behind her, she noticed Roger and Clyde following at a respectable distance. Her stomach churned with unease, but she refused to show any weakness.

Without breaking her stride or looking back again, Miranda focused her attention on the two boys. Taking a deep breath, she willed Roger's shoelaces to become untied and cause him to trip.

"What the!" She heard him exclaim before a string of curses followed.

Miranda couldn't help but smile as she continued walking briskly towards her house. She knew that this small act of revenge would only make things worse in the long run, but it felt good to have some control over the situation for once.

As she approached her front door, Miranda turned around and saw that Roger and Clyde had stopped following her. They were both rubbing their heads with confused expressions on their faces. Miranda chuckled to herself before heading inside.

Miranda's mother met her as she came into the kitchen, concern evident in her voice. "How did things go in school today?" she asked.

"I don't know how to explain it," Miranda replied with a sigh. "Some boys accused me of being a witch."

Her mother's face registered surprise and worry. "Oh my, that is indeed disconcerting. What happened?"

Miranda recounted the events of the day, from the whispers and stares to the confrontation with Roger and Clyde. She left out the part about her telekinetic abilities, not wanting to cause her mother any more worry.

Her mother listened intently and when Miranda finished, she placed a comforting hand on her shoulder. "I'm sorry you had to deal with that today, sweetheart. But remember, those boys' words do not define who you are."

Miranda nodded, feeling grateful for her mother's support. "Miss Stevens interrupted them and told them there was no such thing as witches," she added with a small smile.

Her mother chuckled at this. "I have to hand it to your homeroom teacher, she seems to know exactly what to say and when to say it."

They both laughed at the thought of Miss Stevens using magic against those boys.

"I just hope they leave me alone now," Miranda said with a worried frown.

Her mother's expression turned serious as she looked at her daughter. "If they continue to bother you, we will talk to the principal about it."

"Thanks, Mom," Miranda replied gratefully.

"Now let's focus on something positive," her mother suggested, changing the subject. "Do you have any plans for the weekend?"

Miranda thought for a moment before replying with a shrug. "Not really."

"Would you like to spend some time together? Maybe go see that new Harry Potter movie you've been wanting to see?"

A smile spread across Miranda's face. Spending time with her mother always made her feel better. "I would like that very much. And then thinking to herself *"Maybe Harry can teach me how to use my powers for good.*

Chapter Four – More Discoveries

The following day at school, Miranda felt a newfound confidence in herself, bolstered by her mother's words of encouragement and the prospect of a fun weekend ahead. As she navigated the hallways, the usual whispers and glances seemed to have quieted down, replaced by a sense of intrigue that surrounded her like a protective shield.

During math class, Miranda's pencil suddenly rolled off her desk and fell to the floor. As she leaned down to pick it up, she heard a soft whisper in her mind. "Look under your desk." Startled, Miranda obeyed the voice and discovered a crumpled piece of paper with the words "You're not alone" written on it.

Confusion clouded her thoughts as she glanced around the classroom, but no one seemed to be paying her any attention. After carefully tucking the note into her pocket, Miranda couldn't shake off the feeling that someone was watching over her, guiding her in subtle ways.

As the day went on, Miranda couldn't shake the eerie feeling that she was being watched. The mysterious note hidden under her desk only added to her sense of unease. During lunch break, as Miranda sat alone in a secluded corner of the cafeteria, deep in thought, a shadow fell across her table.

Looking up, she saw Timothy standing there hesitantly, a conflicted expression on his face. Miranda gestured for him to sit down, curiosity piquing her interest.

"I need your help," Timothy blurted out, his voice barely above a whisper.

Miranda studied him intently, noting the desperation in his eyes. "What kind of help do you need?" she asked softly, trying to calm his obvious distress.

Timothy's eyes darted around nervously before he leaned in closer, his voice barely above a whisper. "I overheard Roger and Clyde discussing something...something dangerous. They're planning to pull a cruel prank during the school talent show tomorrow," he said, his hands shaking with fear.

Miranda's heart raced with a mix of unease and determination as she absorbed his words. She knew she had to intervene, to prevent any harm from coming to her classmates. "What exactly are they planning?" she asked urgently, her mind already racing to come up with a solution.

Timothy hesitated, clearly conflicted between wanting to do the right thing and fearing the consequences of betraying his peers. Finally, he spoke in hushed tones, "They want to rig the lights so they'll fall on the stage during someone's performance. It could seriously injure someone."

A chill ran down Miranda's spine at the thought of such a malicious scheme. Without hesitation, she made up her mind. "Thank you for telling me, Timothy. I'll take care of it."

As Timothy nodded gratefully and slipped away, Miranda knew she had to act quickly. She couldn't risk anyone getting hurt because of Roger and Clyde's twisted plan.

She racked her brain for a solution. Should she tell the Principal? But how could she explain how she knew about the plan? The same went for her homeroom teacher. She could confide in her mom, but then what could her mother do without proof?

Desperate for answers, Miranda used her keen sense of observation to search the auditorium, trying to figure out what the boys had done or were planning to do with the lights. But with no prior knowledge or expertise in engineering, her attempts were fruitless.

Next, she considered using her telepathic abilities to read the boys' minds and uncover their plans, but that would expose her powers and potentially put her in danger. She had to think of another way to stop Roger and Clyde before it was too late.

Instead, Miranda decided to take matters into her own hands. She knew she had to act quickly before the talent show started, or worse before anyone got hurt. With a determined look in her eyes, she slipped away from the cafeteria and stealthily made her way toward the auditorium where the show was going to take place.

As Miranda approached the backstage area, she could hear muffled voices and the sound of tools being used. Peeking around a corner, she saw Roger and Clyde huddled together near the lighting control panel, their faces twisted in malicious grins.

Taking a deep breath to steady her nerves, Miranda focused all her energy on the control panel. She closed her eyes and concentrated with all her might, willing the lights to malfunction and prevent Roger and Clyde from carrying out their dangerous plan.

A flicker of electricity crackled in the air, causing Roger and Clyde to look around in confusion. The lights above them sputtered and dimmed before going completely out, plunging the area into darkness.

"Come on let's get out of here, Clyde said. Miranda could hear the boys stumbling over things in the dark as they tried to get away from the scene of their attempted crime.

Later when the janitor came to clean the area, he discovered that the lights were out, and after checking the electrical panel and not finding the reason he decided to notify the school principal and ask him to have the panel checked.

Once again Miranda had saved the day without exposing herself to further scrutiny.

As the school principal arrived at the auditorium, he was met by a bewildered janitor who explained the mysterious blackout. The principal frowned and quickly made his way to the control panel where Miranda still stood, pretending to survey the scene like everyone else.

"What happened here?" the principal asked, his voice filled with concern.

Miranda hesitated for a moment before replying nonchalantly, "I'm not sure, sir. The lights just seemed to malfunction all of a sudden."

The principal nodded thoughtfully, glancing around at the dimly lit stage. "Well, it's fortunate that nobody was hurt. We'll have to get this fixed before the talent show starts." He turned to the janitor and instructed him to contact an electrician immediately.

As the adults bustled around, inspecting the control panel and discussing solutions, Miranda discreetly slipped away from the auditorium. She knew she had done the right thing by stopping Roger and Clyde's dangerous plan, but she also knew that her actions couldn't go unnoticed forever.

With a sense of satisfaction and a touch of apprehension, Miranda decided to keep her heroic deed to herself. The talent show went on without any more disruptions, and as the audience erupted in applause at the end of the night, Miranda smiled quietly to herself, content in knowing that she had once again saved the day – a true unsung hero in the shadows.

As the sun dipped below the horizon, a new chapter was set to begin for Miranda – one filled with hidden powers, mysterious whispers, dangerous plans, and unseen battles. But despite all odds, she remained steadfast, her secret well-guarded behind her innocent smile. After all, she was just a girl named Miranda - not a witch but a girl who happened to have an extraordinary gift.

Chapter Five – Two Years Later

The burden of keeping her secret had become too much for Miranda to bear. She had made the difficult decision to never use her gift again, no matter what the circumstance. This choice had served her well for a time, but on a class nature trip one day, her resolve was put to the test. One of her closest friends announced with distress that she had lost her beloved necklace. Miranda knew how much the necklace meant to her friend - it had been a gift from her father just before he embarked on his deployment to the Middle East.

Miranda's heart pounded in her chest as she stood at the crossroads of morality and loyalty. Her power was a double-edged sword, capable of both protecting and destroying. But at this moment, as she saw tears streaming down her friend's face, she knew what she had to do.

With determination in her eyes, Miranda walked away from the group, desperate to keep her secret hidden. As she closed her eyes, she called upon her power and summoned the bracelet. Beads of sweat formed on her brow as she focused all her energy on the shiny object nestled deep in a crevice above them.

With a fierce intensity, Miranda willed the bracelet to reveal itself to her. The ground began to shake beneath her feet as the prized possession shimmered and shook, rising from its hiding place.

When it reached the top of the crevice, Miranda allowed it to settle to the ground instead of calling it to her hand. The voice in her head was warning her to be careful.

Miranda walked gracefully back to the group, her long strides carrying her effortlessly. She saw Mary Beth huddled in the center, her shoulders shaking with sobs. With a gentle but firm grasp, Miranda wrapped her arm around her friend and willed her to be calm, projecting positivity and strength.

"Where did you last have your bracelet?" she asked, her voice soothing like a lullaby.

Mary Beth furrowed her brow in concentration, and Miranda nudged her mind gently towards the memory of where she had seen the bracelet last. A spark of recognition lit up Mary Beth's face as she pointed up the hill, towards a spot that Miranda knew all too well - it was where the necklace lay waiting to be discovered.

The class monitor, a determined expression etched on her face, led the charge up the hill with unwavering confidence. She rallied the other children, urging them to fan out and keep their eyes peeled for any sign of the missing object. Meanwhile, Miranda stayed back, keeping a hawk-like gaze on two particular children - Roger and Clyde. Suspicion gnawed at her as she couldn't shake off the feeling that they were somehow involved in the disappearance of the precious necklace.

As the children scoured every inch of the area, Miranda's watchful eye caught Roger and Clyde exchanging nervous glances. Their usual cocky demeanor was replaced by unease, making them stand out like sore thumbs among the eager search party. Miranda's suspicions only deepened as she saw them subtly trying to lead the search away from the exact spot where the necklace was hidden. She knew she had to act fast before they could intervene and retrieve the stolen item.

In a quick and calculated move, Miranda used her mind to guide Mary Beth towards her lost necklace. While most of the class was searching the far right of where the necklace was, Mary Beth deftly shifted to the left under Miranda's direction. Roger and Clyde noticed this sudden change and quickly moved to try and get between Mary Beth and the necklace, but it was too late. With a burst of triumph, Mary Beth retrieved her beloved possession, thanks to Miranda's clever intervention.

As Mary Beth clutched her recovered necklace with tears of joy streaming down her face, the class erupted into cheers and applause. The class monitor beamed with pride at the successful resolution of the search, unaware of the crucial role Miranda had played behind the scenes.

Roger and Clyde, on the other hand, watched in silent frustration as their plan unraveled before their eyes. Miranda's gaze bore into them with an intensity that sent shivers down their spines. They knew they had narrowly escaped exposure, but the look in Miranda's eyes warned them that she was not one to be trifled with.

As the excitement died down and the class began to make their way back to the bus, Mary Beth caught Miranda's eye and mouthed a silent "thank you" across the distance between them. Miranda offered her a warm smile in return, a silent understanding passing between the two friends.

At that moment, Miranda realized that her gift was not just a burden to bear but a powerful tool that could help others.

But, then she noticed Roger and Clyde watching her intently. Miranda took a chance and allowed her mind to meld with theirs.

"There was no way that Mary Beth could have found that necklace since I threw it into that crack and I saw it a good 30 feet down. It had to be the witch helping her." Clyde was looking directly at Miranda when he said it.

However, the accusation lingered in Miranda's mind like a dark shadow. She couldn't shake off the feeling of being exposed, vulnerable to the judgment and fear of those around her. The words "witch" echoed in her thoughts, a reminder of the isolation and danger that came with her extraordinary abilities.

Despite her efforts to appear unaffected, Miranda couldn't ignore the growing tension between her and the two troublemakers, Roger and Clyde. Their gazes bore holes into her, filled with suspicion and malice. It was clear they wouldn't let this go easily.

As the class made their way back from the nature trip, Miranda felt a heavy weight settle in her chest. She knew that her secret was no longer safe and that she would have to confront the consequences of her actions sooner rather than later. With each step she took, the world around her seemed to blur as she braced herself for what was to come.

That night she told her mother what had taken place. "You need to be careful how you use your gift. Some people would love to take advantage of what you can do," Her mother told her.

That night as she was sleeping she again had a dream where a ghostly figure came to her and warned her that she needed to keep her gift safe and that she should only use it to help others and never for personal gain.

Chapter Six – Reflections

In the heart of a game of hide and seek, Miranda stood behind a dilapidated oak tree laden with moss, her senses on high alert. Her gift, that beautiful yet laborious anomaly, pulsed within her brain like a beacon, begging to be unleashed. She could detect the faint echoes of laughter from her friends hiding behind an old stone shed to her right and another nestled between giant haystacks to her left. An ordinary child would have to rely on sight, sound, and a bit of luck to win, but Miranda had more at her disposal.

But she didn't succumb to the allure. Each heartbeat was a promise made to herself - an oath she wouldn't break for a simple game. Her fingers traced over the rough bark of the tree as she took a deep breath, grounding herself in reality.

The card games were no less arduous. As she sat around the worn wooden table, a deck of cards clutched in her hand, the temptation rose again - seductive and demanding. She could persuade Tom to discard that King of Spades or make Alice pick up from the pile when she didn't need to. But as she looked at the expectant faces around her and felt the weight of the cards in her hand, she lifted her chin and kept her gift dormant.

A school test was another battle entirely. The small classroom filled with hushed whispers and the scratching of pen on paper was like an arena. Every question was a challenge thrown at her, every blank space on her answer sheet an opponent to defeat. Could she not just skim through Mrs Clarke's mind and find the solutions? The answer sheet sitting within easy reach on Mrs Clarke's desk seemed to taunt her.

Yet Miranda did not falter.

Even as sweat trickled down her forehead and gathered at the corner of her lips, even as the hands of the clock marched relentlessly forward, she held firm. Balancing the weight of her pen delicately between her fingers, she wracked her brain to recall the lessons.

The internal strife Miranda faced was colossal. To possess a gift that could make life so much easier and yet need to stifle it was an enormous struggle. It was like being a bird with the ability to soar high in the sky but being bound by chains, unable to break free.

But in her heart, Miranda knew it was a battle she couldn't afford to lose. For every time she resisted the seductive call of her gift, she grew stronger. She learned discipline and self-control. And above all, she learned that while gifts could define us, they did not have to control us.

So, she stood her ground - from hide-and-seek games in the dusty backyard to card games around the old wooden table and grueling tests at school. Each decision not to use her gift for selfish gains was a victory in itself.

Suddenly, the bell above the schoolhouse door rang out, its high echoes signaling the end of the examination. The room full of students sighed in relief, dropping their pens and leaning back on their chairs.

Miranda placed her pen on top of her answer sheet and straightened in her chair. A quiet determination settled within her as she waited for Mrs Clarke to collect the papers. Her heart pounded in her chest like a triumphant drum - resounding with victory but anticipating battles yet to come.

As Miranda's teenage years unfolded, a new layer of complexity was added to her already challenging existence. Alongside the trials of mastering her telekinetic gift, she found herself drawn to boys in a way that went beyond mere friendship. The innocent kickball games of childhood now gave way to heart-fluttering moments and racing thoughts whenever a certain someone was near.

These newfound romantic feelings, however, proved to be a double-edged sword. As Miranda's emotions swirled and tangled, so did her telekinetic powers. In moments of infatuation, her ability to control objects with her mind faltered, leading to mishaps and surprises that often left her blushing with embarrassment.

The internal battle between her yearning to impress and connect with those she admired and her commitment to using her powers responsibly became a central theme in Miranda's journey. Would she succumb to the temptation to show off or bend the rules to catch someone's eye, risking the exposure of her extraordinary abilities? How would these conflicting desires shape her choices and ultimately define the path she walked as she navigated the turbulent waters of adolescence?

As she walked into the crowded high school dance, Miranda's heart began to race. She couldn't help but notice Jacob, a popular and athletic boy from a grade above her. His toned muscles and effortless charm caught her attention immediately. But as she tried to approach him, doubts crept into her mind. What if he didn't notice her? What if he already had someone else? Despite her yearning for him, Miranda couldn't help but feel conflicted about her feelings for Jacob.

Remembering her gift, she thought of how easy it might be to probe Jacob's mind to see if he had even noticed her, and if he hadn't maybe she could plant such an idea in his mind. But then her mental companion was there to keep her focused on right and wrong.

Miranda's internal struggle between her attraction to Jacob and the ethical use of her powers intensified as the night went on. She found herself stealing glances at him from across the room, admiring his easy smile and the way he effortlessly interacted with everyone around him.

As the music played and the crowd swayed to the rhythm, Jacob finally made his way over to Miranda. Her heart raced, unsure of what to expect. "Hey, Miranda, right?" he said with a friendly grin.

Miranda felt her cheeks flush with color as she nodded in response. "Yeah, that's me."

"I've seen you around school," Jacob continued, oblivious to the whirlwind of emotions going on inside Miranda. "You always seem so focused in class. What's your secret?"

Miranda couldn't help but smile at his words, feeling a flutter of butterflies in her stomach. "I guess I just like to pay attention," she replied shyly.

As they chatted, Miranda's mind raced with conflicting thoughts. On one hand, she was ecstatic that Jacob was talking to her and showing genuine interest. On the other hand, she struggled with the temptation to use her telekinetic powers to make him like her even more. The internal battle threatened to overwhelm her, but she took a deep breath and focused on the present moment.

As they continued their conversation, Miranda found herself opening up to Jacob in a way she had never done before. His easygoing nature and genuine curiosity put her at ease, making her forget about her powers and the weight they carried.

Suddenly, the music shifted to a slow song, and Jacob extended his hand towards Miranda. "Would you like to dance?" he asked with a warm smile.

Miranda's heart skipped a beat as she placed her hand in his and let him lead her to the center of the dance floor. As they swayed to the music, Miranda felt a sense of peace wash over her. At that moment, nothing else mattered but the simple joy of being with Jacob. She let herself get lost in the music and the warmth of his hand on her waist, feeling a connection that transcended words or thoughts.

As they danced, Miranda's powers remained dormant, overshadowed by the genuine emotions swirling inside her. She realized that she didn't need to rely on her telekinetic abilities to form a bond with someone; she could just be herself and let things unfold naturally.

Jacob looked into her eyes, his gaze intense yet tender. "Miranda, I have to admit something," he began, his voice barely above a whisper over the music.

Caught off guard, Miranda's heart raced with anticipation. "What is it?" she asked, her voice barely audible in return.

"I've always admired you from afar," Jacob confessed, his cheeks turning a faint shade of pink. "Your intelligence, your kindness... there's something about you that draws me in."

Miranda felt a rush of emotions at his words, a mixture of disbelief and elation washing over her. She never imagined that Jacob, the popular and charismatic boy she secretly admired, would feel the same way about her. As she searched his eyes for any sign of insincerity, she found only honesty and vulnerability.

"I-I don't know what to say," Miranda stammered, her heart pounding in her chest. Her mind raced with a million thoughts at once, trying to make sense of this unexpected confession.

Jacob gently lifted her chin with his finger, tilting her face towards his. "You don't have to say anything," he whispered, his breath warm against her skin. "Just know that I meant every word."

At that moment, surrounded by the soft melody of the music and the gentle glow of the dimmed lights, Miranda felt a newfound sense of courage welling up inside her. She leaned in slowly, closing the gap between them as their lips met in a tender kiss.

But little did she know that this special moment would be spoiled by two old nemesis. The lights suddenly went out, plunging the dance floor into darkness and causing confusion and panic among the students. Miranda remembered when Roger and Clyde had messed with the lights at school and she was immediately suspicious that they might be involved with this event as well. Now she used her powers to reach out to the two troublemakers to see what they had done with the lighting.

Miranda's hands tingled as she focused her telekinetic energy, reaching out into the darkness to seek out Roger and Clyde. She sensed their presence nearby, a mischievous aura emanating from the pair. With a surge of determination, Miranda honed in on their location and directed her powers toward them.

In the shadows, Roger and Clyde were snickering to themselves, reveling in the chaos they had caused. However, their laughter was cut short as they felt an unseen force grip them tightly, lifting them off the ground. Panic washed over their faces as they realized they were no longer in control.

Miranda's voice echoed through the darkness, her words laced with authority. "Roger, Clyde, enough is enough. You will not ruin this dance with your pranks."

She held them in place, making sure they couldn't move an inch. The other students, still engulfed in darkness, were unaware of the supernatural showdown happening right under their noses. Roger and Clyde squirmed and protested, their voices filled with fear as they realized they were at the mercy of Miranda's powers.

"Let us go, Miranda!" Roger cried out, his voice tinged with desperation. "We didn't mean to cause any harm."

Clyde nodded frantically, his eyes wide with terror. "Please, we'll never pull another prank again, we swear!"

Miranda's grip remained firm as she glared at the two troublemakers. "You've caused enough trouble for one night," she stated firmly. "It's time you both learned your lesson. Turn the lights back on and then leave this gymnasium and don't think about coming back."

Roger and Clyde exchanged nervous glances, realizing they were no match for Miranda's formidable powers. With a reluctant nod, they fumbled to restore the lights in the gymnasium, casting a dim glow over the dance floor once more. The students let out a collective sigh of relief as the music resumed and the party atmosphere returned.

As Roger and Clyde scurried out of the gym, chastened by Miranda's display of authority, she released them from her telekinetic hold. They stumbled away, shooting her one last resentful look before disappearing into the night. Miranda could sense their frustration and embarrassment, but she knew it was necessary to stand up to their antics and protect her fellow classmates from further disruptions.

Turning back to the dance floor, Miranda found Jacob waiting for her with a concerned expression. "Are you okay?" he asked, his eyes searching hers for any sign of distress.

Miranda offered him a reassuring smile, feeling a rush of gratitude for his unwavering support.

Never before had Miranda used so much effort not even when she broke up the altercation between Roger, Clyda, and Timothy. She could barely get her breath." Yes, I guess I am just a little tired. Thank you for the dance. I hope we can do it again sometime."

As Jacob took Miranda's hand in his, a wave of relief washed over her. In that moment, surrounded by the fading echoes of the music and the lingering tension from the earlier confrontation, she felt a sense of peace settle within her.

"Anytime," Jacob replied with a gentle smile, squeezing her hand reassuringly. "I'll always be here for you."

Miranda nodded, grateful for his understanding and unwavering presence. As they swayed together on the dance floor, the troubles of the night seemed to melt away, replaced by a quiet sense of connection and camaraderie.

The dimly lit gymnasium faded into the background as Miranda focused on the steady rhythm of their movements, finding solace in the simple act of dancing with someone who truly cared. With each step they took together, Miranda felt a renewed sense of strength and determination building within her.

As the song came to an end and the last notes hung in the air, Miranda looked up at Jacob with a soft smile. "Thank you," she whispered, her eyes reflecting a mixture of gratitude and something deeper – a growing bond between them that transcended words.

As Miranda strolled through the high school corridors on Monday morning, she noticed Roger and Clyde engaged in a conversation with her newfound friend, Jacob. Preferring not to engage with the troublemakers, she simply waved at Jacob in a friendly manner as she passed by.

"Is it true?" Jacob inquired.

"True? If it's from those two, I highly doubt its credibility," Miranda responded.

"Did you cause the lights to go out on Friday night?" Jacob pressed.

"Jacob, you were with me the whole time. How could I have been responsible for the lights?" Miranda countered.

"They're saying you're a witch," Jacob revealed.

Miranda looked at him with a mix of disdain and sadness. "And do you believe them?" she questioned.

"How old are you, Jacob?" Miranda quizzed.

"Almost 15. Why?" Jacob answered.

"Aren't you a bit too old to be believing in witches?" Miranda quipped.

Upon entering her homeroom class, Miranda was informed by her teacher that she was requested in the Principal's office. Despite questioning the reason, her teacher remained tight-lipped. Without further delay, Miranda made her way down to the first floor and headed towards the Principal's office.

Approaching the counter, she introduced herself to the student advisor on duty and explained the purpose of her visit. Afterward, she was instructed to take a seat and assured that she would be called in when the time came.

A short while later Miranda was told that the Principal would see her now. As she entered the inner office the Principal looked up and gestured for her to take a seat across from his desk.

"I guess you know why you are here?" the Principal asked.

"Not a clue," Miranda replied and then regretted her short answer.

"It has been reported to me that you were the one that caused the lights to go out at the school dance on Friday. Would you like to tell me why you would do such a thing?"

"I will tell you that what was reported is not true. I was on the dance floor when the lights went out and thus I had no opportunity to do anything with the lights."

"Then why do you think someone would say that you did?"

"I can imagine that the person or persons might be named Roger or Clyde. And I further imagine that they were the ones that messed with the lights. Did you ask them where they were when the lights went out?"

The Principal looked down as if avoiding answering Miranda's question.

"I will look into this further," the Principal finally replied, his expression unreadable. "Thank you for your cooperation, Miranda. You are free to go back to class."

Miranda nodded, her mind racing with frustration at the unfair accusation that had been leveled against her. As she left the Principal's office and made her way back to homeroom, she couldn't shake the feeling of being unjustly targeted by Roger and Clyde once again.

Throughout the day, whispers and sidelong glances followed Miranda wherever she went. She could sense the rumors spreading like wildfire, painting her as a troublemaker and a witch in the eyes of her classmates. The weight of their judgment bore down on her, but she refused to let it break her spirit.

Determined to clear her name and put an end to the malicious gossip, Miranda sought out Jacob during lunch break. She found him sitting alone at their usual table, his expression troubled as he glanced up at her approach.

"Jacob, we need to talk," she said.

"I don't know what we have to talk about," Jacob replied.

"I am sorry I bothered you. I just thought you might tell me why you would take the word of two of the school's biggest troublemakers over mine. If you will recall we had just shared a kiss when the lights went out. What reason would I have for causing trouble at the dance?"

Miranda could see the realization dawning on Jacob's face as her words sank in. He shifted uncomfortably in his seat, clearly torn between believing the rumors and trusting Miranda. After a moment of silence, he finally spoke up.

"I... I'm sorry, Miranda. I didn't mean to doubt you. It's just that with all the stories going around about your powers and what happened at the dance, I didn't know what to think," Jacob confessed, looking sheepish.

Miranda softened at his admission, understanding the pressure he must have felt caught between loyalty and gossip. "It's okay, Jacob. I know it must be hard to separate fact from fiction, especially with Roger and Clyde spreading lies about me," she reassured him.

Just then Roger and Clyde walked by the table that Miranda and Jacob were sitting at.

Clyde's warning to Jacob struck a nerve with Miranda, causing her to lose her composure. With a surge of her telekinetic abilities, she attempted to visualize Clyde transforming into a toad. While the transformation didn't occur, she succeeded in prompting Clyde to confess and apologize for his actions with Roger at the dance. Coincidentally, the Principal happened to be passing by and intervened, leading Clyde and Roger to his office for further discussion.

Chapter Seven – Miranda's Journey Without Power

That night, as Miranda drifted off to sleep, the ethereal figure visited her once more in a dream. It solemnly explained that due to her attempt to exploit her powers for personal gain, they were being stripped away from her.

Upon awakening the next morning, the remnants of the dream lingered vividly in Miranda's mind. Eager to test her newfound reality, she reached out to move a teddy bear from a shelf using her telekinetic abilities, only to be met with silence and stillness. Despite the initial wave of sadness at the loss of her powers, Miranda's emotions shifted as she reflected on the burdens her secret had carried.

In the following days, Miranda discovered a surprising development – though her telekinesis was gone, her cognitive abilities seemed to have sharpened. Previously attuned to thoughts, she now found herself adept at deciphering people's emotions through subtler cues: a twitch of the lips, a tightening of the jaw, or a shift in posture spoke volumes to her newfound perception.

While not a human lie detector, Miranda's heightened sensitivity allowed her to sense evasion in responses, catching the nuances of hesitation and revealing more about those around her than she ever imagined possible.

As Miranda refrained from using her telekinetic abilities to excel academically, her dedication to genuine effort and hard work flourished. With her powers now a distant memory, she dove headfirst into her studies, fueled by a newfound determination to succeed through sheer perseverance.

Her enhanced focus and unwavering discipline set her apart in the classroom. Miranda's sharpened study habits, coupled with her heightened cognitive abilities, allowed her to absorb and retain information with remarkable clarity. While her classmates struggled to grasp complex concepts, Miranda effortlessly synthesized and understood intricate subject matter, often surpassing their academic achievements with ease.

The once daunting prospect of examinations now transformed into opportunities for Miranda to showcase her exceptional knowledge and understanding. Her exemplary performance on tests and assignments became a testament to her unwavering commitment to learning and self-improvement, earning her accolades and admiration from teachers and peers alike.

Through her dedication and resilience, Miranda not only excelled academically but also discovered a newfound sense of fulfillment and pride in her accomplishments.

By the time graduation came Miranda had excelled to the position of Valedictorian. As she stood at the podium in her Black Cap and Gown, she spoke of the marvels that her classmates were about to embark on.

Dear graduates, esteemed teachers, dedicated staff, supportive parents, and beloved friends,

As we gather here today on the cusp of a new chapter, I am filled with gratitude for the incredible journey we have shared. Our high school years have been a tapestry woven with the threads of growth, challenges, friendships, and cherished memories. To each teacher who ignited our curiosity, every staff member who supported our endeavors, our parents who stood by us, and friends who shared in our joys and sorrows – I offer my heartfelt thanks for being the guiding lights on our path to success.

Reflecting on our collective journey, I am reminded of the diverse tapestry that is our graduating class. We celebrate the beauty of our differences and the strength that comes from understanding and appreciating one another. Let us embrace open-mindedness and the valuable lessons that stem from learning from the unique perspectives each of us brings to the table.

Our high school experience has been a testament to resilience and perseverance in the face of challenges. Let us draw inspiration from those among us who conquered adversity to achieve remarkable success, showing us that setbacks are merely opportunities for growth and transformation.

Looking forward, I urge each of you to face the future with optimism and purpose. Whether your path leads to higher education, vocational training, or the workforce, remember the importance of lifelong learning beyond the confines of the classroom. Curiosity and adaptability will be your allies in navigating the ever-changing landscape of the world around us.

As we stand on the threshold of new beginnings, remember that the choices you make today will shape the course of your future. Let responsible decision-making and ethical behavior be your guiding principles, steering you toward a future of integrity and fulfillment. Together, we are a powerful force, and through unity and collaboration, we can achieve remarkable feats.

In celebrating our achievements and unique strengths, let us carry forward the torch of making a positive impact on the world. Each of you possesses extraordinary talents and gifts – use them to leave an indelible mark on the world around you.

In conclusion, my fellow graduates, I implore you to see today not as an end, but as a commencement. Embrace the opportunities that lie ahead with courage and determination, for the world eagerly awaits the transformative impact that every one of you will undoubtedly make.

Congratulations, graduates! The world is yours to shape and change for the better.

Epilogue

The theme of recognizing the magical powers within ourselves and the ability to transport to wondrous realms through the magic of books is profoundly captivating. Imagine the limitless potential that resides within our minds, akin to the vast expanse of magical abilities Miranda possessed. Just like her, we have the power to shape our reality, influence our surroundings, and impact those around us.

By delving into the world of literature, we unlock doors to fantastical realms, travel to distant lands, and immerse ourselves in the lives of diverse characters. Books are indeed portals to boundless adventures, where our minds can soar beyond the constraints of reality and explore the depths of imagination.

Through the lens of this theme, we are encouraged to reflect on how we harness our internal magic. Do we wield our abilities for the greater good, as Miranda chose to do, or do we sometimes find ourselves tempted by selfish desires? It prompts us to contemplate the ethical use of our powers, whether they be literal or metaphorical, and the impact they have on our lives and those around us.

Every time we open a book, we embark on a journey that transcends time and space, allowing us to broaden our horizons, gain new perspectives, and tap into the reservoir of knowledge and wisdom that lies within the pages. Our brains, indeed the most powerful of computers, hold the key to unlocking a treasure trove of experiences, insights, and dreams waiting to be realized.

So, as we navigate the intricacies of our lives, let us remember the enchanting magic that resides within us and the transformative power of storytelling. Through the act of reading and learning, we empower ourselves to shape our destinies, inspire others, and create a world brimming with wonder, compassion, and boundless possibilities.

Book 2 - Miranda's Child

Chapter One Tim's Time Twisting Find

Timothy was named after a boy that his mother, Miranda had befriended way back in grade school. While they had remained friends through the years, Miranda had married one of her high-school sweethearts. Jacob.

When Timothy was born, Miranda could feel something emanating from him and she thought about her own magic which she had lost as she entered puberty. But as the years passed, Timothy only displayed the same kind of magic that all young children possess, that of curiosity.

As Timothy grew older, Miranda couldn't shake off the feeling that there was something special about him. Despite his lack of overt magical abilities, she sensed a deep connection between Timothy and the mystical world she had once known.

Miranda often found herself reminiscing about her childhood adventures with magic, wondering if Timothy would ever experience the same wonders. She wondered if her own lost magic could somehow be passed down to him, dormant and waiting to awaken.

Meanwhile, Timothy's curiosity continued to drive him, leading him to endless explorations of the world around him. He was fascinated by nature, spending hours in the backyard observing insects, plants, and animals. Miranda watched him with a mixture of pride and longing, wishing she could share her own magical experiences with him.

One day, while Timothy was playing in the woods behind their house, he stumbled upon an ancient-looking book hidden beneath a tangle of roots. Intrigued, he carefully brushed away the dirt and leaves to reveal the title: "The Book of Lost Magic."

Excitedly, Timothy brought the book home to show Miranda. As she flipped through its pages, Miranda felt a surge of nostalgia wash over her. The spells and incantations within were familiar yet distant, like echoes of a forgotten dream.

Together, mother and son delved into the secrets of the book, experimenting with spells and charms in their backyard. With each discovery, Miranda felt a glimmer of hope reignite within her—a hope that Timothy might inherit more than just her love for magic.

Little did they know, their playful experiments would soon awaken ancient forces long dormant, setting into motion a chain of events that would change their lives forever.

Chapter Two-The Discovery

Timothy's knees creaked as he shuffled across the wooden floorboards of the attic, his fingers skimming over the cobwebbed surfaces of forgotten memories. The musty air was thick with dust motes dancing in the slanting beams of light that filtered through the small windows. Everywhere he looked, relics of the past teetered in precarious piles: books with cracked spines, photographs that had faded to ghosts of their former selves, and toys that had long since lost their laughter.

"Come on, there's got to be something here," Timothy murmured to himself, his voice a low whisper in the silence of the attic.

He pushed aside a moth-eaten coat that might have been fashionable several decades ago and continued his search. A glint caught his eye—a metallic sheen winking at him from between two leather-bound tomes that hadn't felt the tender caress of human hands in ages.

"Hello, what's this?" His heart quickened its beat, a drumroll of excitement that filled the cramped space.

Kneeling before the shelf, Timothy's breath hitched as he reached out, his hand trembling slightly. The metal object was wedged tight, but with a gentle tug, it came free, sending a cascade of dust particles swirling around him like tiny golden fireflies.

"Gotcha!" he exclaimed, his voice echoing off the walls as if the attic itself shared in his triumph.

His eyes sparkled with the reflection of his find, the corners of his mouth curving upwards into an eager grin. Though he didn't yet know the significance of what he held in his hand, the weight of potential destiny seemed to pulse against his skin.

Timothy cradled the ancient pocket watch in his palm, a shiver of anticipation crawling up his spine. "What secrets do you hold?" he whispered to the timepiece as if expecting it to whisper back.

The watch felt oddly warm, its temperature rising against his skin, sending a gentle vibration of energy through his body. His fingers tingled as he caressed the smooth, cold metal, and for a moment, Timothy wondered if the watch was somehow alive, its heartbeat syncing with his own.

"Look at these engravings," he marveled softly, tilting the watch this way and that as the dim light from the attic window danced over its surface. The patterns were like nothing Timothy had ever seen, swirls and symbols intertwining in an elegant dance of silver on brass. It was as though each line, each curve held the echo of an ancient story, waiting for just the right person to come along and read it.

"Dragons, castles, and... is that a phoenix?" Timothy traced the delicate image of a bird ablaze with fire, reborn from its ashes. "Incredible." His eyes, wide with wonder, followed the lines of a castle turret down to a mighty dragon curled protectively around it.

"Gosh, where did you come from?" He narrowed his eyes, hoping to spot some sort of signature or mark from whoever crafted it, but it stayed hidden, making the little trinket even more mysterious.

"Feels like holding history in my hands," he mused, the weight of the watch both comforting and daunting. This wasn't just some trinket; it was a key to times long past, an invitation to an adventure Timothy felt he was born to embark upon.

Timothy's thumb, hesitant yet compelled, toyed with the dial of the pocket watch. It was an almost imperceptible movement, a mere nudge really, but the effect was immediate and astonishing. A shiver ran through the air, a whisper of movement that raised the fine hairs on the back of his neck.

"Whoa," he breathed out, eyes darting around the attic as he tried to make sense of what had just happened. The dust motes that floated lazily in the shafts of light seemed to quiver expectantly.

"Did you feel that?" Timothy asked the silence, half expecting an answer from the shadows that lurked in the corners of the room. There was none, of course, but the charged atmosphere seemed to beg for dialogue, for someone to acknowledge the change that was taking place.

He twisted the dial again, a bit more boldly this time, and the ticking—the steady heartbeat of the watch—heightened in volume, crescendoing until it filled the space, echoing off the walls and drowning out the distant sound of suburbia that filtered through the attic window.

"Okay, okay, not imagining it." His voice came out a touch too loud, trying to compete with the symphony of ticks and tocks that surrounded him. He glanced over his shoulder, half-expecting to see some spectral figure approving his bravado or warning him of danger. But it was just him, Timothy, alone with a relic that defied logic.

His fingers paused, hovering over the dial. Should he dare? Yes, he should. With a firmer twist, reality bent. The room blurred like a photograph caught in motion, edges smearing into streaks of color as if the very fabric of time were being stirred by an invisible spoon.

"Wow!" His voice filled with awe, a mix of excitement and a hint of fear that sent shivers down his spine. "This... this can't be real..."

But it was. As the world steadied itself, Timothy felt the certainty settle in his chest. This was real. The pocket watch was more than an artifact; it was a tool, one that he now held. And with every tick, with every tock, with every breath he took, he understood that he had stumbled upon something extraordinary.

"Time," he murmured, the word soft but full of magic. "You listen to me now."

Timothy's hand, trembling with the weight of possibility, turned the dial left. A motley of dust motes hung suspended in a beam of sunlight, frozen like stars in an unmoving galaxy. He exhaled sharply, the sound unnaturally loud in the stillness.

"Wow," he whispered, looking around the attic in amazement. He saw a spider, frozen in the middle of climbing its web, its legs completely still. "Is time standing still?"

Timothy controlled time with the turn of a dial. He reveled in its power, pausing, rewinding, fast-forwarding at his command. The world obeyed, objects and memories retracing their steps before his eyes. Timothy was time's keeper now, his fingers dancing with newfound grace. Every second was his to mold, and he relished the thrill of it all.

back with unanswered questions: What were its limits? Who made it and why? And most importantly, what would it mean for his future?

"Too much power... It's intoxicating." Emotion cracked in his voice as he grappled with joy and fear of manipulating time.

"Can I trust myself with this?" Timothy stared at the watch, now still after his command. He felt a kinship with its frozen hands, loaded with potential and consequence.

"Fulfill your purpose," he told the pocket watch. "I will uncover your secrets and learn where you came from."

With one last glance around the attic where it all began, Timothy placed the watch in his pocket and descended the ladder. Each step was a commitment to his journey for knowledge.

"I'll find the answers," he declared as he stepped into a changed world. With the weight of the watch by his side, he dove into unraveling the mystery of his destiny one tick at a time.

Chapter Three-Call To Action

Timothy's heart was a drumline, rapid and thundering as he burst through the doorway. The pocket watch felt like a living thing in his palm, its cold metal vibrating with an energy that seemed to pulse in time with his excitement. He skidded across the polished wooden floor of his mother's room, his breaths coming out in quick, eager gasps.

"Mom!" he exclaimed, words tumbling over each other in his haste. The golden heirloom watch glinted in the soft light streaming through the curtains, drawing a line of radiance across his flushed face.

Miranda turned from her vanity, an eyebrow arching in response to her son's unbridled enthusiasm. "Timothy? What on earth has gotten into you?"

He opened his mouth, then closed it, suddenly aware of the weight of what he had discovered. Timothy glanced down at the gleaming artifact in his hand, feeling the intricate engravings beneath his fingertips. How could he begin to explain the magic that seemed to whisper to him from within its gears?

"Mom," he started again, his voice a mix of wonder and hesitation. "In the attic... I found something. Something incredible."

The pocket watch seemed to hum louder, urging him to reveal its secrets. Timothy knew this moment was not just about what he held, but about crossing a threshold into a world he had only ever dreamed of.

Miranda's book, a hefty tome of ancient lore, slipped noiselessly onto the plush comforter as her son's words hung in the air. A lock of auburn hair tumbled loose from behind her ear as she leaned forward, her eyes reflecting a spark of interest that mirrored the gleam of the pocket watch.

"Something incredible?" Miranda echoed, her voice soft but edged with a keenness that beckoned him closer. "Show me, Timothy."

He approached tentatively, the carpet muting his steps, and extended the watch towards her. The metal seemed to shimmer unnaturally as if reluctant to be parted from its new keeper.

"It's more than just old or valuable," Timothy murmured, his gaze entranced by the ticking hands. "When I touched it, there was this... this surge. Like electricity, but alive, whispering secrets."

"Secrets?" Miranda probed gently, encouraging yet careful not to rush the torrent of revelations.

Timothy nodded, swallowing the lump in his throat. "I can't explain it. Time, sort of... bends around it. And when I concentrate, really focus on the ticking, I can slow it down, speed it up. I even stopped it once!" His chest heaved with a mixture of pride and trepidation. "Is that even possible?"

"Anything is possible," she replied with a curious tilt of her head, a smile touching her lips. "Especially for those who believe in the impossible."

"Is that why you always told me tales of sorcerers and time weavers before bed? So I would believe?" His voice wavered between excitement and doubt.

"Perhaps," Miranda conceded with a twinkle in her eye. "Or perhaps I sensed something special within you, waiting for the right moment to awaken."

"Then you're not mad?" Timothy's question was laced with the hopeful innocence of youth.

"Mad?" She chuckled warmly and shook her head. "No, my dear boy, I'm intrigued. And very proud. You have stumbled upon a gift—a rare and powerful one."

The glow of the afternoon sun seemed to wrap them both in an ethereal embrace as Timothy absorbed her words. He felt the comforting warmth of acceptance wash over him, emboldening his spirit.

"Can you teach me, Mom? How to use it responsibly?" His eyes shone with determination.

"Of course, Timothy." Miranda's voice was a soft caress, a promise. "We'll explore this path together."

"Thank you," he whispered, feeling the weight of destiny settling upon his shoulders, lighter now with his mother by his side.

The room was silent, save for the soft ticking of the pocket watch that Timothy held out before him. Its hands moved in reverse, a dance against time choreographed by the subtle gestures of his fingers.

"Mom," he muttered, his brow furrowed in concentration as he demonstrated the impossible. "Look."

Miranda's eyes were riveted to the spectacle, her breath caught somewhere between her heart and her lips. She leaned forward, her posture mirroring the intensity of her son's focus. As she watched the delicate second hand move backward, an understanding dawned on her, bright and sharp as a shard of glass catching sunlight.

"Timothy," she whispered, her voice tinged with a mixture of astonishment and recognition. "This...energy you're channeling. I've felt something like it before."

He paused, the watch ceasing its backward march at the sound of her voice. "You have?"

"Yes." She reached out, not to the watch, but to gently touch his cheek, as if to assure herself of his reality. "When I was about your age, strange things began to happen around me. Books would fly off shelves, and doors slammed shut without a breeze. At first, I thought they were just coincidences, but then I realized there was more to it."

"More to it?" Timothy echoed, a universe of questions swirling in his eyes.

"Telekinesis," Miranda said, the word falling from her like a secret finally set free. "My emotions, my thoughts—they could move objects. It started small, but grew stronger with time."

His mouth opened slightly, a silent 'o' of wonder at the revelation. The watch in his hand felt suddenly heavier, a tangible link to this new, shared heritage.

"Can you still—" he began, but trailed off, unsure how to finish the question.

"Not anymore" she admitted with a gentle nod. "I learned to control it, to keep it hidden. Powers like ours, they can be misunderstood, feared even."

"Then we're the same," Timothy breathed, a smile dawning like the first light of daybreak upon his features. "Different, but...the same."

"Exactly," Miranda confirmed, returning his smile with one that mirrored the pride and love she felt for her son. "And together, we'll learn to harness these gifts. To use them wisely."

"Wow..." Timothy let out a long exhale, a mix of relief and excitement coursing through him. He looked down at the watch, then back to his mother. "It's a lot to take in."

"Indeed, it is," she agreed, her hand now resting atop his, enveloping both the watch and his smaller fingers in a warm embrace. "But remember, Timothy, we are bound by more than blood. We are kindred spirits, touched by the extraordinary."

"Kindred spirits," he repeated, the phrase anchoring him amidst the tide of revelations. "I like the sound of that."

"Me too, my dear boy, me too."

The revelation rippled through Timothy like a shockwave, his gaze locking onto Miranda's with an intensity that belied the confusion and wonder swirling within him. "You... all this time? You've had powers too?" The words tumbled out in a hushed awe, as if saying them louder might shatter the fragile tapestry of normalcy they'd lived until now.

"More than you know," Miranda said softly, her voice holding a depth that spoke of untold stories. Her eyes, usually so full of warmth, carried a glint of old storms weathered alone. She reached across to squeeze his hand, anchoring him to the moment. "To keep such a secret is not easy, my son. There were times I felt isolated by what I could do, afraid of how the world would react."

"Isolated..." Timothy echoed, the weight of the word pressing down on him. He tried to picture his mother, young and uncertain, grappling with an invisible force that set her apart from everyone else.

"Sounds terrifying," he murmured, scarcely imagining his gentle mother at the mercy of such raw, unpredictable power.

"It was," she admitted, allowing herself a moment of vulnerability in front of her son. Her eyes briefly closed, as if she could still see the fragments of her past scattered before her. "But over time, I learned control, discipline. I realized that with great power comes an even greater need for responsibility."

"Responsibility?" The word rolled around in Timothy's mind, heavy with implications he was only just beginning to grasp.

"Absolutely," Miranda confirmed, opening her eyes to meet his with an unflinching resolve. "Powers like ours can change things. They can help, but they can also harm, even when we don't mean them to. You must be mindful, always, of the consequences of your actions."

"Consequences..." Timothy's grip on the pocket watch tightened reflexively. He understood now the gravity of what lay ahead, the care he would have to take with each tick and tock within his newfound domain.

"Timothy," Miranda's tone softened, "you have a gift, a remarkable one. But remember, it doesn't define you. You choose who you want to be, with or without this power."

He looked up at her, seeing not just his mother but a mentor, a guide through the labyrinth of their shared legacy. In her eyes, he found not only warnings but also a wellspring of support.

"Thank you," he whispered. With those simple words, he stepped forward into a world larger than he'd ever known, yet comforted by the bond that linked them beyond mere flesh and blood—they were kindred spirits, indeed.

Timothy paced the length of his mother's room, the ancient pocket watch cool against his palm. He stopped abruptly and turned to face Miranda, who watched him with a patient gaze.

"Mom, I need to understand this—how to use it," he said, his voice determined yet edged with a hint of trepidation. "I want to do good with it, not just... not just let it be some... freaky accident."

Miranda leaned forward, her hands clasping together as if to gather the weight of his words. "You have a noble heart, Timothy. To wield such power for the sake of others is the mark of true strength."

"But how?" Timothy's brow furrowed in concentration. "How did you learn to control what you can do?"

"Through practice, patience, and sometimes," Miranda said, a wistful smile touching her lips, "through mistakes. But those are lessons too."

"Then teach me," he pleaded, his eyes alight with the fire of youth and desire for purpose.

Miranda rose from her seat, her presence like a beacon in the dimly lit room. She placed her hand gently upon his shoulder, grounding him. "It would be my honor," she said, her voice thick with emotion. "And we'll learn more together than apart. You're not alone in this journey, Timothy."

"Really?" His voice cracked slightly, revealing the hopeful child beneath the burgeoning guardian of time.

"Really," she confirmed, pulling him into an embrace that fortified their bond. "We'll navigate this path side by side."

"Thank you, Mom." Timothy held onto her, the watch between them—a silent promise of the adventures and trials that lay ahead.

Timothy paced the room, his excitement is palpable as he turned to face Miranda. "So where do we start? What's our goal?"

"First," Miranda began, her gaze steady and sure, "we master the watch. We need to understand every nuance of its power, and how it resonates with your own."

"Okay, mastery first. Then what?" Timothy asked, his hands animatedly gesturing as if he could already grasp the future they were planning.

"Then," she continued, the corners of her mouth lifting with a shared sense of adventure, "we use it to help people. Discreetly, of course. There are moments in time, pivotal seconds that shape lives—maybe we're meant to ensure they turn out right."

"That sounds... incredible." Timothy's voice was tinged with a mix of awe and determination. "We could be like secret guardians of fate."

"Exactly!" Miranda exclaimed, her eyes dancing with the reflection of their lofty aspirations. "But we must tread carefully. With such powers come great responsibilities—and risks."

"Risks?" His forehead creased with concern.

"Indeed," she nodded gravely, "which is why secrecy is paramount. Not everyone will understand or welcome our gifts."

A moment of silence passed between them, filled with the heavy weight of their impending pact.

"Then we agree," Timothy said, a newfound maturity seeping into his tone, "to keep our powers hidden from the world. To protect others, and ourselves, from what could happen if they fell into the wrong hands."

"Agreed," Miranda affirmed, her voice low but firm. The gravity of their vow seemed to solidify in the air around them, binding them to a path only they could walk together.

"Promise me, Mom," Timothy pressed earnestly, his youthful eyes locking onto hers, seeking assurance beyond words.

"Timothy, I promise. On this journey and beyond, our secret remains our strength," she pledged, extending her hand to him.

With a solemn nod, he took her hand, their fingers intertwining—a tangible symbol of their unity and resolve. They stood there, mother and son, united by blood and now by a deeper covenant, ready to face whatever their extraordinary destiny had in store.

Chapter Four The Magic Shop

The bell above the door chimed melodically as it swung open, announcing Timothy and Miranda's entrance into a realm where the mundane world seemed to fall away. They stepped over the threshold, and the air buzzed with an energy that prickled their skin, a subtle promise of secrets waiting to be unearthed.

"Whoa," Timothy breathed out, his eyes darting across the cornucopia of curiosities that lined the walls and shelves of the shop. Glass jars filled with swirling mists sat alongside ancient tomes bound in leather that whispered of forgotten spells. A constellation of small, twinkling lights floated near the ceiling, casting a soft glow over the room.

"Look at this place," Miranda murmured, her voice hushed in reverence as she trailed her fingers over a row of vials that shimmered with iridescent liquids. Each potion beckoned with its own silent siren call, promising effects that were wondrous or perilous, or perhaps both.

"Can I help you find something?" The voice was smooth like velvet and carried the weight of knowledge hard-earned through years unfathomable to the young visitors.

Timothy turned, catching sight of Sylvia for the first time. She exuded a calm authority, her silver hair cascading down her shoulders like a moonlit waterfall. Her piercing blue eyes seemed to see right through them, discerning their innermost thoughts with a single glance.

"We're... uh, looking for some information," Timothy stammered, momentarily caught in the intensity of Sylvia's gaze.

Sylvia offered a gentle smile, which softened the sharpness of her features and made her seem less like a sentinel guarding arcane secrets and more like someone who had seen much but still found joy in guiding the uninitiated. "Information is one of the many things this shop provides," she said, gesturing for them to come closer to the counter where she stood in quiet command of her domain.

"Thank you," Miranda said, her curiosity painting her tone with excitement as they approached the counter, stepping into the circle of wisdom that seemed to radiate from Sylvia.

"Let's begin," Sylvia said, her eyes glinting with the spark of untold stories, eager to unlock the potential she saw hidden within these two young souls standing before her.

"Welcome to the threshold of the arcane," Sylvia greeted, her voice a soothing balm to the uneasy flutter in Timothy's chest. "What mystery brings you across my doorstep today?"

Miranda nudged Timothy with her elbow, urging him to find his voice. He swallowed the lump in his throat, the pocket watch an anchor in his pocket, grounding him to the moment.

"Ms. Sylvia," he began, his words initially a shaky whisper that grew steadier with each syllable. "We need your help. I found something... unusual."

"Ah," she said, leaning forward with genuine interest, her blue eyes reflecting a lifetime of secrets unearthed. "Tell me about this discovery."

"It's a pocket watch," Timothy said, his fingers twitching towards the heirloom concealed within his jacket. "But not just any watch—it does things. Impossible things."

"Go on," Sylvia prompted, her tone encouraging yet tinged with the seriousness of one who understands the gravity of such items.

"It seems to be able to stop time," he confessed, feeling a peculiar mix of fear and exhilaration wash over him as he shared the secret. "When I hold it, when I really concentrate, I can... move time. It's like the world pauses and listens to it."

"Moves time, you say?" Sylvia repeated, her gaze sharpening, not with skepticism, but with a recognition that sent shivers down Timothy's spine. "A rare ability indeed. A dangerous one if left unchecked."

Timothy nodded, the reality of her words weighing heavily upon him. Miranda reached out, placing a comforting hand on his shoulder. They stood united, ready to learn, to understand the weight of the power that had fallen into their hands.

"May I?" Sylvia's voice was a soft whisper, her hands outstretched in anticipation.

"Of course," Timothy replied, and with great care, he slipped his hand into the pocket of his jacket. He pulled out the ancient pocket watch, its surface gleaming dimly in the shop's mystical light. The artifact seemed almost alive as he placed it gently on the open palm of his outstretched hand for Sylvia to see.

"Remarkable," she breathed. The silver wisps of her hair seemed to quiver with excitement as her eyes, bright as sapphires, drank in every detail of the watch. "The craftsmanship is exquisite."

Timothy watched as Sylvia leaned closer, her gaze never leaving the pocket watch. She extended a slender finger, adorned with rings that held their secrets, and lightly traced the elaborate engravings etched into the watch's golden surface. Each symbol and pattern held the echo of an ancient time, whispering tales of forgotten magic and hidden realms.

"Curious..." Sylvia murmured, half to herself. Her lips moved silently as if reciting words from a long-lost language, and her expression was one of intense concentration. "Very curious indeed."

Timothy exchanged a puzzled look with Miranda, who shrugged slightly, equally entranced by Sylvia's reaction. They both knew, at that moment, that they had found someone who could unlock the mysteries wrapped tightly around the pocket watch's timeless dance.

Sylvia's fingers paused in their delicate dance over the watch, and she lifted her gaze to meet Timothy's anxious eyes. The corners of her mouth curled into a knowing smile, one that seemed to hold centuries of secrets.

"Timothy, Miranda," she said, her voice a melodious tune that resonated through the quiet hum of the shop. "This is no ordinary trinket you've stumbled upon. It sings with an ancient power, thrumming with abilities that are unique in this world or any other."

Timothy swallowed hard, his fingers twitching at his side as if the watch still rested within his grasp. "Unique how?" he managed to ask, his voice barely above a whisper.

"Unique in a way that defies time itself," Sylvia replied, her blue eyes gleaming with a light that seemed to mirror the stars. "It's as if the universe has conspired to entrust you with a fragment of its very essence."

The air around them felt charged, each word from Sylvia weaving an invisible tapestry of possibility and wonder. Miranda, who had been standing silently by Timothy's side, leaned forward, her curiosity piqued.

"Are you saying we can learn to use it?" she asked, her tone tinged with both skepticism and hope.

"Indeed," Sylvia affirmed, clasping her hands together as if sealing an unspoken pact. "And I would be honored to guide you on this path. To teach you the art of harnessing the energies that slumber within that pocket watch."

"Us?" Timothy interjected, incredulity lacing his words. "But we're...we're just ordinary people."

"Ordinary?" Sylvia chuckled softly, the sound like chimes in a gentle breeze. "No one who crosses the threshold of my shop is ever 'just' anything, dear boy. You, Timothy, and you, Miranda, have the potential to wield magic, to become adept in ways many can only dream of."

Timothy felt a surge of excitement course through him, a wave crashing against the shores of his doubt. Beside him, Miranda's eyes shone with a mixture of pride and wonder. "Will you accept my offer?" Sylvia asked, her expression earnest as she awaited their answer.

Timothy's heart skipped a beat, his gaze locking with Miranda's as they silently communicated a world of emotions. With a glance that shimmered with unspoken stories, they nodded to each other, an alliance forming in that shared look. The air between them crackled, charged with the potential of what was to come.

"Ms. Sylvia," Timothy began, his voice steadier than he felt, "we'd be fools to pass on this. We accept your guidance with open arms." His words tumbled out, eager and sincere.

Her piercing blue eyes bore into theirs, leaving no room for doubt about the gravity of her words. "This journey will test you in ways you cannot yet imagine. But fear not," Sylvia continued, her tone imbued with an unyielding resolve, "for I shall lend my strength to yours. Together, we will uncover the secrets locked within that ancient timepiece."

"Whatever it takes," Timothy replied, the determination settling into his bones like a second skin. He felt Miranda's hand squeeze his shoulder, her silent affirmation merging with his own.

Sylvia's silver hair shimmered as she navigated through the labyrinth of shelves, her robe trailing behind her like a river of moonlight. The air buzzed with the muted whispers of ancient charms and jars filled with ingredients that winked at Timothy and Miranda as they passed

"Here we shall begin," Sylvia announced, gesturing to the space cleared of clutter, save for a worn table and two chairs. "Timothy, sit. Miranda, stand beside him. There is much to learn, and our time, though bendable, is precious."

She directed Timothy to a chair, where he sat with his back straight, the pocket watch heavy with secrets resting in his palm. Miranda hovered close, her eyes tracing the intricate patterns that danced across the walls, etched in the shadows cast by the undulating candlelight.

"Close your eyes, Timothy," Sylvia instructed, her voice a soft command that seemed to resonate from the very stones beneath their feet. "Let go of the tangible world around you. Feel the pulse of the watch, its rhythm synchronizing with your heartbeat." And with that, she began to relate all she could about the magical realm that she was about to open.

As they left the shop, the door chimes sang a farewell, their crystalline notes escorting them into the night. Beneath the cloak of stars, mother and son shared a look of mutual anticipation. The journey ahead brimmed with mysteries and perils, but also with the hope of untold wonders, and together, they stepped into the embrace of the unknown.

Chapter Five-Training and First Challenge

Sylvia's steps whispered softly over the fallen leaves, her slender silhouette weaving between the ancient oaks. Timothy trailed behind, his breath misting the crisp air of the training grounds. Magic lingered here, a subtle thrum that harmonized with the earth's pulse.

"This spot," Sylvia declared, her voice clear as the babbling brook nearby, "shall be our sanctuary."

Timothy surveyed the tranquil clearing, feeling the weight of centuries in the whispering winds and rustling leaves. Here, time seemed to stand still, holding secrets of ages past.

"Ready, Timothy?" Sylvia's emerald eyes met his, brimming with anticipation.

He nodded, reverence in his gesture, as Sylvia placed the pocket watch in his outstretched hands. Its cool weight pulsed with latent power, symbols etched upon its surface seeming to dance in the dappled light.

"Focus," Sylvia instructed, her tone a blend of command and encouragement. "Let it awaken."

As Timothy concentrated, the watch responded, humming with a resonance that spoke of bending moments and expanding horizons.

"Can you feel it?" Sylvia's voice tingled with excitement. "The energy it holds?"

"Yes," Timothy whispered, awe coloring his voice. "It's... alive."

Sylvia's enigmatic smile conveyed both pride and encouragement. "That's the spirit of time you're sensing—ancient, boundless, waiting for you to learn its dance."

Timothy's excitement surged. Here, under Sylvia's guidance, he stood on the cusp of understanding a power many deemed fantastical.

"Time isn't a river," Sylvia's voice rang out, cutting through the grove's tranquility. "It's a vast sea, and you are its navigator."

Timothy nodded, his grip on the watch tightening as Sylvia's words resonated within him.

"Focus is your compass," Sylvia continued, her gaze locking onto his with unwavering intensity. "And intention, the wind in your sails."

The weight of Sylvia's teachings settled upon Timothy. Mastery over time beckoned, but with it, the specter of responsibility loomed.

"Observe," Sylvia instructed, opening her watch to reveal its intricate workings. Timothy watched, mesmerized, as Sylvia attuned herself to the flow of time.

"Listen," Sylvia whispered, her voice melding with the ticking of the watch. "Become one with the moment."

Timothy's breath slowed, aligning with the rhythmic cadence of the ticking. Sylvia's demonstration unveiled a world beyond his comprehension, yet tantalizingly within reach.

"The watch is both a tool and teacher," Sylvia reminded him, closing her watch and returning to the present moment.

"Respect and diligence," Timothy echoed, acknowledging the weight of the responsibility now his to bear.

Gratitude swelled within Timothy as he looked at Sylvia, the dappled sunlight casting her in an ethereal glow.

"Thank you," Timothy began, sincerity imbuing his words. "For everything. This... exceeds my wildest dreams."

Sylvia's smile mirrored the warmth of the sunlight filtering through the leaves. "You possess a rare spark, Timothy. Nurture it well."

Her hand, a comforting presence on his shoulder, conveyed belief in his potential.

"Trust in yourself," Sylvia urged her voice a beacon in the gathering shadows. "And let the watch be your guide."

Timothy nodded, determination firming his resolve. With each beat of the watch, he felt the pulse of time coursing through him.

"Keeper of time," Sylvia said, bestowing the mantle upon him. "Its steward."

Timothy accepted the responsibility, feeling the weight of destiny settle upon his shoulders.

As the sun dipped below the horizon, Timothy stepped forward, the fading light casting his shadow long and resolute behind him. His journey with the magical pocket watch had begun, his spirit unyielding in the face of the challenges ahead.

Chapter Six-Good Deeds

As Timothy and his mother exited the shop, a weighty silence enveloped them, each lost in their contemplation. Miranda's mind drifted to memories of her past, recalling the days when she wielded her powers for good, until that fateful encounter with Clyde and Roger. The sadness that followed her awakening the next morning, bereft of her abilities, still lingered.

Unaware of his mother's inner turmoil, Timothy walked beside her, his thoughts consumed by the possibilities the pocket watch held. It seemed to pulse with potential in his pocket, beckoning him to imagine the ways he could use it.

Sensing his eagerness, Miranda gently reminded him that he couldn't rush things. Patience, she emphasized, was key. The opportunities to utilize the watch's power would present themselves in due time. All he needed to do was remain vigilant and receptive. The power would be there when he truly needed it.

As they neared their home, Timothy heard the blaring of a horn and looked up just in time to see a gray cat about to be run over by a car.

Without even thinking of what he was doing he twisted the dial of the watch and time stopped with the cat only inches from the tires of what was a speeding car. Timothy quickly ran over and grabbed the cat pulling it to safety. When he returned to his mother with the cat, Timothy again twisted the knob, and time returned to normal.

"Wow, that was a close one," Timothy said to his mother.

"It sure was, Mrs. Jenkins would have been heartbroken if you hadn't saved her cat. How did you manage to act so quickly?"

"I don't know, mom. It was as if the watch was telling me what to do."

"Come on let's take Whiskers back to Mrs. Jenkins."

Mrs. Jenkins took her cat and thanked Miranda and Timothy for bringing him back safely to her. Neither Miranda nor Timothy mentioned the close call that Whiskers had had as it would have been hard to explain how the rescue occurred.

The morning sun cast long shadows across the bustling street as Miranda and Timothy made their way to the bank. A sense of urgency tingled in Miranda's bones, urging her to finally cash those long-neglected checks. Timothy, off from school for spring break, tagged along, his thoughts drifting towards the promise of a lunchtime pizza if things went smoothly.

As they entered the bank, joining the line, the atmosphere shifted abruptly. A gut-wrenching scream shattered the mundane hum of transactions. Panic spread like wildfire as a voice barked orders, demanding compliance with the threat of violence. Miranda and Timothy exchanged a tense glance, each sensing the other's fear in the charged air.

Drawing on dormant abilities, Miranda focused her mind, reaching out to Timothy with a silent command to remain calm and utilize the watch. A ripple of acknowledgment brushed against her consciousness as time seemed to halt, leaving her suspended along with the other patrons, save for Timothy.

In the eerie stillness, Timothy moved with a quiet determination, his every step deliberate. With swift precision, he disarmed the robbers, relieving them of their weapons and placing them at their feet, a silent act of defiance against the frozen tableau of fear.

Outside, the silent alarm had summoned help, and the distant wail of sirens promised imminent rescue. Timothy knew they couldn't leave everyone frozen until the authorities arrived; the explanations would be too convoluted. With a twist of the dial on the watch, time resumed its steady march just as the first police officer breached the bank's entrance.

The scene that greeted the officers was one of confusion and disbelief. Instead of armed criminals menacing the hostages, they found them disarmed and subdued, thanks to the quick thinking of a young boy who wielded time itself as his ally.

As the chaos of the attempted robbery dissolved into the reassuring presence of law enforcement, Miranda and Timothy exchanged a knowing glance, a silent acknowledgment of their shared secret.

With the situation under control, the officers began to question witnesses and assess the aftermath. Timothy and Miranda remained composed, offering their accounts of the events with a measured honesty that belied the extraordinary nature of their intervention.

As the officers began to wrap up their investigation and assure the safety of the bank's patrons, Miranda and Timothy took their leave, slipping away from the scene with a sense of quiet satisfaction. They knew that their actions had made a difference, and that was enough.

Back at home, as they settled into the familiar comforts of their surroundings, Miranda turned to Timothy with a smile that held a trace of wistfulness.

"You did well today, Timothy. You've proven that you have the courage and the wisdom to wield your gift responsibly."

Timothy returned her smile, a spark of determination lighting his eyes.

"I'll do my best, Mom. With great power comes great responsibility, right? But I couldn't have done it without you and your power to push thoughts into my mind."

Miranda's smile widened, a proud warmth filling her heart.

As the sun began its descent, casting warm hues across the tranquil neighborhood, Miranda and Timothy found solace in the familiarity of their home. The events of the day had brought them closer together, reinforcing their bond as they navigated the uncharted waters of wielding magic in a world unaware of its existence.

Sitting together in the comforting embrace of their living room, they reflected on the events that had unfolded—the close call with Whiskers, the daring rescue at the bank, and the quiet courage Timothy had displayed in the face of danger.

As the evening wore on, a sense of peace settled over them, tempered by the knowledge that their journey was far from over. With each passing day, they would continue to hone their abilities, learning to navigate the complexities of their newfound powers with grace and humility.

But amidst the uncertainties that lay ahead, one thing remained steadfast—the unbreakable bond between mother and son, forged in the crucible of shared challenges and triumphs. Together, they would face whatever the future held, drawing strength from the love and support that bound them together.

And as the day gave way to night, enveloping them in its gentle embrace, Miranda and Timothy found solace in the knowledge that, no matter what trials lay ahead, they would face them together, united in purpose and bound by a love that transcended time itself.

The end

Did you love *Miranda's Gift*? Then you should read *I Wish I Was a Cowboy*[1] by Wayne Simmes!

[2]

A man dies and then comes back to life in a different time and different place. He soon discovers that he is in what he believes to be the old west, although he has no idea what territory or time frame he is in. He wonders how all this is possible, and then he meets a stranger that seems to be some type of guide.

---

1. https://books2read.com/u/meKowg

2. https://books2read.com/u/meKowg

Also by Wayne Simmes

The Devil, The Ghost and Will Anderson
I Wish I Was a Cowboy
I Never Thought I Would Live This Long
Tales of Romance and Infidelity
Wive's Fury Unleashed - Two Tales of Betrayal and Retribution
The Rustlers of the Sonoran Desert
Miranda's Gift

About the Author

With a literary career spanning an impressive three decades, Wayne Simmes is a seasoned writer whose words reflect the tapestry of a life rich in experiences. Born in a quaint small town in western New York State, Wayne Simmes draws inspiration from the landscapes of their youth and the unique charm of close-knit communities.

Throughout the majority of his life, Wayne Simmes has been immersed in the dynamic world of sales, bringing a profound understanding of human interactions, negotiations, and the nuances of relationships to his writing. This background adds a layer of authenticity to his storytelling, allowing readers to connect with characters navigating the complexities of life, love, and ambition.

At the age of 79, Wayne Simmes continues to be a prolific force in the literary world, weaving tales that resonate with the wisdom only garnered through years of lived experiences. His work reflects a keen observation of the ever-changing world, coupled with a timeless understanding of human nature.

www.ingramcontent.com/pod-product-compliance
Lightning Source LLC
Chambersburg PA
CBHW060449160726
47992CB00003B/1147